You C[an't Have]
a Party Anywhere!

Written by Jill Eggleton
Illustrated by Dylan Coburn

Tom put on the silver spacesuit and looked in the mirror.

"I look goofy," he said to his mom.

"No you don't," said his mom. "You will be the coolest kid at the party."

But the truck started to make a funny noise.
Tom's mom stopped the truck
and looked at the engine.

She went

tap, tap, tap.

"It'll be OK now," she said.

But it wasn't. The old truck went slower and slower. Soon there was a long line of cars behind them.

The noise got louder and louder. Then there was an **enormous**

bang

and a big black cloud of smoke came puffing out of the engine.

Tom's mom stopped the truck right in the middle of the road. The car behind had to stop in a hurry. All the cars in the line had to stop in a hurry. Horns went

toot, toot, toot,

and people shouted,

"Get that old truck off the road!"

Tom and his mom got out of the truck.
People were shouting and waving their arms.

A big man with a big smile and a red beard
came up to Tom's mom.

"Hi," he said. "I'm Red."

He took out his cell phone.

"I'll get some help," he said.

11

Tom felt really goofy in his silver suit.
He tried to hide behind the truck,
but Red saw him.

"Why are you in that suit?" he asked.

"I was going to a party," said Tom.

Red laughed and tugged his beard.
"You can have a party anywhere!"
he said.

Red went away and got a guitar.
He sat up on the old truck and he sang.
The people stopped shouting,
and they started to sing, too.

A woman came along with bags of chips.
"If we are having a party," she said,
"we will need some food."

When the police came, they saw people laughing and talking and eating chips. They saw a big man in a red beard playing a guitar, and a boy in a silver suit hopping and bopping around an old truck.

"Look at that," said the police.
"You can have a party anywhere!"